THE JACK REACHER CASES (THE MAN WHOSE AIM IS TRUE)

DAN AMES

Slogan Books, New York, NY

PRAISE FOR DAN AMES

"Fast-paced, engaging, original."

— NEW YORK TIMES BESTSELLING AUTHOR THOMAS PERRY

"Ames is a sensation among readers who love fast-paced thrillers."

— MYSTERY TRIBUNE

"Cuts like a knife."

— SAVANNAH MORNING NEWS

"Furiously paced. Great action."

— NEW YORK TIMES BESTSELLING AUTHOR BEN LIEBERMAN

A USA TODAY BESTSELLING BOOK

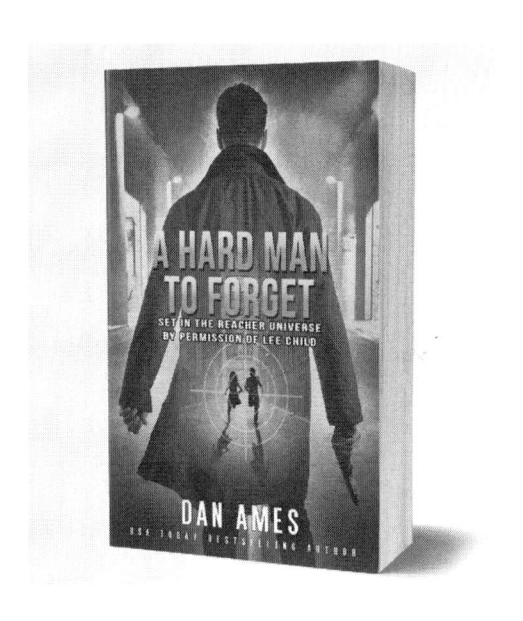

Book One in The JACK REACHER Cases

AUTHORDANAMES.COM

FREE BOOKS AND MORE

Would you like a FREE copy of my story BULLET RIVER and the chance to win a free Kindle?

Then sign up for the DAN AMES BOOK CLUB:

AUTHORDANAMES.COM

THE MAN WHOSE AIM IS TRUE

The Jack Reacher Cases #15

by

Dan Ames

**But from each crime are born bullets
that one
day seek out in you where the heart lies.**
-Pablo Neruda

CHAPTER ONE

Moments before his head was blown apart by a sniper's perfectly placed bullet, the older man opened the gate to the dog park.

He was probably in his early sixties, wearing dark brown corduroy pants, a heavy sweater and a black jacket, unzipped. Although his shoulders were stooped, he had a keen, clear gaze and moved with a quiet confidence.

The dog park was a tiny square of green bordered on all sides by rows of neat and highly desirable Brooklyn brownstones. At one end was a set of picnic tables and a second, fenced-in area for larger dogs. At several locations were cylindrical waste baskets and plastic bags designed to deal with by-products from man's best friend.

The sky was baby blue tinged with mile-high borders of cirrus streaks, and a faint breeze blew the few remaining strands of white hair lazily above the old man's ears. It was cool, but not cold and the sounds of several dogs barking punctuated the otherwise serene-like setting.

The Schipperke Terrier on the end of the old man's leash was happy to see his old friend, an Italian Greyhound named Sal who was about his same size. He strained against his leash, eager to get inside the fence and start the best part of his day.

When the bullet hit – a custom round larger and more powerful than its nearest relative, the .300 Winchester Magnum, traveling at nearly 2,800 feet per second – the little dog both felt and heard the impact. The Schipperke's name was Churchy, named after the old man's idol Winston Churchill. Churchy had never heard that particular sound before and suddenly the firmness on the other end of the leash was gone.

The smell of blood reached the dog's nose and something primal triggered his fear. He darted back to his owner who was now on the ground. Churchy barked, but it was as if no one could hear him.

He kept barking but the man he viewed as the

leader of their pack, remained still. The smell was something unique to Churchy.

A high-pitched scream startled the dog, and soon, there were more screams and shouts and then a high-pitched wailing followed by flashing red lights.

Churchy had a feeling he wouldn't be playing with his friend today, after all.

CHAPTER TWO

War criminal.

Lauren Pauling stared at the words on her computer screen. She sat in her home office, in her loft on Barrow Street in New York City. Her hair was pulled back and she hadn't changed out of her workout clothes: yoga pants and a sports bra.

Pauling had been going through her email, which to her surprise, hadn't slowed down even after the sale of her security firm. As often as she unsubscribed from junk email, it seemed there were new ones ready to replace them.

Once she discarded all of the trash messages, she finally opened the one email she actually wanted to read. It was from an old friend at her former place of employment: the Federal Bureau of Investigation.

Pauling hadn't been with the FBI for years now; in fact, she'd started, built and sold her firm in the intervening time period. But she still kept in touch with some of her colleagues. A few, actually, as in very few.

But Deborah Haskins had been one of her best friends. Pauling had been her senior and she'd mentored Haskins and the two had grown very close. Haskins was probably nearing the end of her career with the Bureau, something Pauling knew her friend was viewing with mixed feelings.

Pauling read the email and sat back in her chair, stunned.

She read it a second time.

There were two words and a name that had shocked her.

The words were *war criminal*.

They certainly weren't new to Pauling. She'd targeted, arrested and helped put away more than a few war criminals in her lifetime.

No, those two words weren't what had given her a shock, enough to drain the blood from her face.

It was the name that followed.

Jack Reacher.

CHAPTER THREE

Within moments of verifying through his rifle scope that the old man's head had indeed been blown into many different directions, the sniper calmly disassembled his one-of-a-kind rifle and placed it in a very generic-looking backpack.

This was not the sort of throwaway weapon one left at the scene to avoid being tied to the crime by authorities.

Not considering how much time, money and effort had been put into designing and customizing the rifle.

The cool, detached demeanor required to make the shot was beginning to dissolve in the shooter's mind. This kill hadn't been an anonymous Taliban fighter in the mountains of Afghanistan.

This kill had meant something.

Emotion, which was something snipers were trained to keep locked down under all circumstances, was beginning to show.

He walked calmly from the rooftop to the access door, then descended the stairs that led to the rear of the building.

As he pushed open the metal door he heard the first of the sirens. This was New York, after all. A man's head getting blown off in a crowded dog park would not go unnoticed for long. The man walked calmly down the alley and turned to his right along the street, away from the kill site.

He had on a black baseball cap, blue jeans, black steel-toed boots and a three-quarters length olive green jacket. He'd slipped on a pair of mirrored aviator sunglasses. His beard was neatly trimmed. He was tall, but not strikingly so, and solidly built, but not overly muscular. To the untrained eye, he simply looked like a well-built, athletic man dressed in a fairly nondescript way.

The rental car was parked on a side street devoid of any bank or store cameras pointed at the street. He'd made sure to put enough time on the meter to avoid being flagged by a traffic cop for a parking ticket and leaving any trace of his presence.

The shooter unlocked the driver's side door and placed the backpack in the passenger seat. He could've put it in the trunk, but he preferred to keep it close to him. Old habits died hard and if need be, he wanted to be able to grab his pack and go, not fumble with the trunk fob.

The sniper was known as Rider, although that was a nickname bestowed upon him in his youth, due to a local legend about a ghost that haunted a legendary, remote road far from the small town in which he grew up. The ghost was rumored to be able to change shape and appearance at will, and was blamed for several strange deaths that had occurred in the town over the years.

No one knew the origin of the name, but the prevailing rumor was that it was the name of a young man who'd been murdered in the 1800s and now haunted the area.

Rider had chosen the name as his sniper handle in the military, although most didn't know its origin.

That was fine with him.

Anonymity was key.

As he drove the rental car away from the

scene, he felt a surge of satisfaction, and a blood thirst.

It was a thirst that would soon be quenched again.

Because Rider was just getting started.

CHAPTER FOUR

After an exchange of emails with her former colleague at the Bureau, Pauling arranged a meeting over a cup of coffee to discuss the ridiculous story that Jack Reacher may have committed a war crime.

The place was called Perk Avenue and was only a few blocks from Pauling's loft. It was a neighborhood joint with a few tables on the sidewalk, and a half-dozen inside. Pauling chose the table at the back of the restaurant out of habit. She rarely felt comfortable dining outside, unless it was a courtyard-type setting or perhaps a café in a small town. There was something about the combination of being somewhat compromised when dining and also sitting so close to the busy streets of New York that didn't mesh well with Pauling.

When she was discussing matters that could possibly land herself or a current employee of the FBI into murky waters, she definitely chose the most private option available.

Special Agent Deborah Haskins entered the coffee shop, ordered an espresso and joined Pauling at the table.

"Pauling," Haskins said.

"Hey," Pauling said. Her friend was a tall, willowy brunette with a lean face and a sharp nose. There were touches of gray in her hair and Pauling couldn't help but think about the deadly combination of sexism and ageism that sometimes occurred at the Bureau. It was much better now, but early in Pauling's career, it had been rampant.

Haskins had survived this long and Pauling knew the woman was bright, assertive and ambitious. She was also principled which sometimes caused issues in the short term but Pauling was optimistic enough to believe in the long run, it was the only way to go.

"You look good. Retirement suits you," Haskins said. Pauling had kept her friend up to date with her post-Bureau life; the firm she'd sold and now, a sort of limbo that technically was retirement. In Pauling's mind, she would never actually retire. She was simply waiting for something to steer her to her next passion.

Her mind naturally went to Michael Tallon, her current significant other, who was presently at his small ranch near Death Valley.

"Thanks, idle hands, as they say," Pauling smiled.

They each sipped the drink – Pauling had opted for a latte.

"How are things at the office?" Pauling asked. She wasn't particularly interested in the usual shenanigans and politics associated with life in the FBI, but she didn't want to dive right into the real reason for the meeting just yet.

Haskins filled her in on her current case: a shady hedge fund manager who was most likely laundering money for a Russian oligarch.

"How about you?" Haskins asked after she'd given Pauling all of the sordid details of the case, including a private jet filled with underage Russian girls.

"I've had a few interesting things come up but lately it's been quiet. The calm before the storm, maybe, based on your message."

Pauling was referring to Haskins' message that someone had claimed Jack Reacher was a war criminal.

"Very strange, that one," Haskins said. "So here's what happened: I'd flagged a whole bunch of stuff related to the Russian oligarch I'm investigating. He had ties to Afghanistan, including some reputed bounties placed on both US and UK soldiers."

Haskins sipped her espresso and leveled her gaze at Pauling.

"One of my alerts tripped a communiqué in Russian that seemed to imply an American soldier was guilty, or at least accused of, war crimes," Haskins explained. "He was in the Army. An MP. And his name was Jack Reacher."

Pauling shook her head. "Impossible, but tell me what else you learned."

"Honestly, not much," Haskins said. "It seems that someone at some point was investigating war crimes committed by Army soldiers, most likely in Afghanistan, although that wasn't totally clear. What those actual crimes were, if they were even actually committed, wasn't included. Nothing else really was."

"It seems much more likely to me that Reacher was the one *investigating* the crimes.

After all, that's what he did in the Army," Pauling pointed out. "He was for all intents and purposes a homicide investigator. And besides, I know him and there was no way he would be involved in that kind of thing as a participant. An investigator sure, but a participant, no."

Haskins pulled a slip of paper from her purse. "I transposed this by hand because I didn't want to send it to the printer."

Pauling knew what she meant: printing something at the FBI meant it was permanently in the record. If the document ever became an issue, it could be traced straight back to the computer that had sent it to the printer.

"Obviously, I know about your history with Reacher so that's why I contacted you," Haskins said. "I also did a quick check of Reacher's record – there's no sign of any active investigation. In fact, his file has been totally inactive for years now."

Pauling nodded. She had told Haskins about Reacher, an indication of how close they'd been. The bond was still there, thankfully.

Pauling slid the note into her pocket.

"Thank you, Deb," Pauling said. "I appreciate it."

Haskins smiled and polished off her espresso. She got to her feet. "No problem. I figure if anyone can get to the bottom of it, you can."

Pauling smiled back.

"That's exactly what I'm going to do."

CHAPTER FIVE

NYPD homicide detective Claire Brewster studied the crime scene and shook her head. She was one of the most consistent cops on the homicide squad when it came to keeping up on the range. She knew her weapons, her ballistics and the many calculations required to estimate the type of kill she was looking at.

As she studied the crime scene at the dog park, where an older man had clearly been shot in the head by a very powerful weapon, she considered the evidence.

It was the power of the weapon that surprised her. A ten-year veteran of the homicide squad, Claire was no stranger to violent crime. She'd been a cop all her life, raised by two

Irish parents who believed in law and order. Her ex-husband could testify to Claire's passion for the job. It was her absence around the house that, according to him, had triggered his departure. Although Claire figured it was the new secretary at his firm that had been the icing on the cake.

"What the hell was this guy using, an elephant gun?" she asked the crime scene tech, a slim Asian man named Kev. She didn't know if that was short for something, or a nickname or maybe she was mispronouncing it, but she didn't care enough to ask. Plus, these days everyone was offended by anything related to one's nationality, so Claire left it alone.

"All I can tell you is that it wasn't a .50 cal. I've seen a couple of those and there would be nothing left," Kev said. His voice was high and raspy, like a female lounge singer from the Fifties.

"It couldn't have been that much smaller," Claire said. "This is more damage than I think I've ever seen."

"Not even close for me," Kev said. "One time, a guy went to Home Depot and brought back a wood chipper to get rid of his roommate. They lived together in a studio apartment. Talk about avant-garde decorating."

The crime scene tech giggled and Claire ignored him.

"How soon will we have ballistics?"

"Considering the situation, I expect this case will be pushed to the top."

Claire knew what he meant; an old man shot down in a dog park, probably by a man with a rifle, was certain to make news. Public scrutiny brought a certain motivation to the political machinery of the NYPD.

Kev finished processing the scene and soon the body was hauled away. Claire worked the witnesses again, and did some door to door. A woman with a Standard Poodle said she'd been walking toward the old man because he was notorious for not picking up his dog's poop. She had intended to confront the issue when the man's head had literally disintegrated in a shower of blood, flesh and bone. Obviously, the woman explained, she felt no need to be concerned after that.

On the bright side, Claire had been able to learn the identity of the victim: one Victor Panko, who lived less than three blocks from the park.

Claire drove her unmarked car to the old man's Brooklyn brownstone. *Nice digs*, she thought.

The front door was locked and no one answered the doorbell. No neighbors came out to check. Claire rang the bell on each neighbor's house but no one answered those, either.

She walked around to the back. There was no garage but instead, a parking space directly behind the building. Parked there was an old Lincoln sedan. Silver. At least fifteen years old but clean. Claire guessed it had low miles and that the engine still packed a punch. She was sure it belonged to Panko – the Lincoln was an old man's car if she'd ever seen one.

She jotted down the license plate and sent it in for confirmation.

Claire wished there was a way she could get inside, but she would have to wait. Until then, she would have to find out all she could about Victor Panko and why someone would want to blow off his head with a high-powered rifle.

She put her car into gear and headed back toward the office.

CHAPTER SIX

The feeling was familiar: frustration.

Ever since Lauren Pauling had met and fallen hard for Jack Reacher, she'd felt a vague sense of frustration. It wasn't that she was still in love with him – in fact, their time together had been so brief that she wasn't even sure she'd had *time* to fall in love with him.

No, Pauling was confident she'd never actually completed that arc; Reacher had stormed into her life and then simply walked out of it. Even back then, she was a mature woman, smart enough and experienced enough to know that he wasn't the kind of man to settle down behind a white picket fence.

Still, no one had ever so completely disappeared from her life like Jack Reacher. He had no fixed address. No car. No cell phone. Certainly no computer and, therefore, wasn't on any type of social media. Hell, Reacher probably hadn't even heard of Facebook or Twitter.

The only real way to trace Reacher was to maybe track down his ATM withdrawals, but that required supreme effort in getting into a bank's records and Pauling had no desire to do that, just yet. It would have to be a dire emergency to take that step.

Pauling wasn't about to panic on Reacher's behalf just because his name had been mentioned in connection with a war crime. In fact, the cool head she still possessed from her time with the Bureau pointed out she had no information there was even an active investigation into possible crimes against her favorite wanderer. Just an intercepted message, chatter over a wire, about something that possibly occurred, but also just as plausibly hadn't taken place.

Having said that, Pauling wasn't the type of woman to ignore it. She still felt connected enough to Reacher and if someone she cared about was possibly being linked to heinous crimes, Pauling wasn't about to wash her hands of the information.

Besides, as Haskins had pointed out, she was retired.

Tallon was at his ranch, and she had spent the last month focused on exercising, eating right and spending time at the range. She loved to shoot and had been experimenting with a new gun: a Colt single action army revolver nicknamed the "Peacemaker."

Deep in her heart, however, she knew she needed something more serious to tackle, and this strange development with Reacher, as unfortunate as it was, fit the bill.

Pauling went back to her loft and headed straight for her home office. It was a small space tucked at one end of the apartment and was outfitted for privacy. She'd had a desk custom made and a wall unit that housed her library as well as several locked compartments for her weapons.

Now, Pauling pulled herself up to her desktop computer and fired it up. Like any organized investigator, she already had a file on Reacher. It had basically been a place to collect the documents from when they had worked together, briefly, years ago. Since then, she'd occasionally received word of some of his escapades and downloaded any notation of them and copied them into the folder.

What she was interested in now, though, was his service record. That, too, was on her desktop in a folder creatively labeled "Reacher."

She opened the documents and reread them, although there was nothing new. She'd spent probably way too much time reading them after he'd gone. He'd been an exemplary investigator, which she already knew, and had climbed the ranks until he'd had a minor setback and then, a few years later, he'd been 'made redundant' as they say.

What interested Pauling was any sign that Reacher had been in Afghanistan.

She scoured all of the paperwork in his file and came to a very clear answer: he had not.

Inwardly, she sighed a small amount of relief. Pauling knew there was no way in hell Reacher was a war criminal, the man was an overgrown boy scout, always doing the right thing and helping out those in need. Reacher hated bullies, had an intense dislike of them so much that he often punched them into the next universe.

Still, it bothered Pauling that someone had made the suggestion.

And why had they?

Pauling knew what she had to do next: study Reacher's cases, or those of his unit. Maybe they had been involved in Afghanistan, without Reacher's involvement.

For that, she would have to go beyond her own desktop folder.

She would have to access records in the Pentagon.

Thankfully, she knew just the person to help her.

CHAPTER SEVEN

Detective Claire Brewster stood on the rooftop and watched the dog park in the distance. According to Kev, based on caliber of the bullet, trajectory at impact, and blood splatter, the shooter had been most likely on this rooftop.

It was a building like any other in New York: the ground floor held some retail shops and the rest were overpriced apartments. The rooftop held nothing but a few exhaust vents, gravel, and pigeon crap.

The problem for Claire was that nothing else had been found on the rooftop by the crime scene techs. They'd already dusted and photographed and measured, but to no avail. They'd found literally nothing, save for one possible foot scrape near the spot where the shooter may have set up his rifle. It was the slightest scuff, black, probably from a boot. They had photographed it, but there wasn't much else they could do. A million kinds of shoes, sneakers or boots could make a mark like that. And the fact that it was only an inch or so from the ground level meant nothing in terms of giving any indication into the shooter's size.

Claire tamped down her frustration and grabbed her iPad. She scrolled through the ballistics report that had just arrived.

It made for interesting reading. The caliber of bullet was still undetermined, but the ballistics expert, a man named Dawson, had put forth a theory that it was a Russian round, rarely used, and somewhat experimental. It was loosely known by an acronym RKN74. The report didn't explain what the hell that acronym stood for but Claire made a mental note to find out.

In some ways, that was good news. The more unusual the weapon or ammo, the easier it would be to trace. "Easier" being a relative term. Simply put, it was better than the bullet being a .223, a .30-06 or a .308 Winchester. The most common sniper rifle in the world, Claire knew, was a 700 Remington (renamed the M24 by the military).

Still, the rifle was unknown. Claire would have

to talk to the weapons expert and find out what kind of rifle could fire this RKN74.

In the meantime, she had work to do. If the shooter had chosen this spot, then it meant that he'd scouted Victor Panko's habits and knew the old man took his dog to the park every day. Which meant the shooter must have spent some time here. She went back down to the lobby and studied the directory.

It was an apartment building with some retail shops on the first floor. There was a guitar repair shop, nail salon and a real estate office. She talked to the owners of all three and got nowhere.

Next, she went into the lobby and sat. As residents walked in with bags of groceries or shopping bags, or even better, dogs, Claire asked them if they'd seen a man in the past few days or weeks who seemed out of place. Especially one with any kind of bag, or a long, rectangular case.

No one knew anything.

Until the old lady appeared out of nowhere. She had on a pink fur coat and carried a white poodle.

"Yes, indeed I saw a young man here two days in a row," the old lady said.

Claire got out her notebook.

"I said hello to him and he nodded back," the

old lady continued. "Didn't say a word, and he didn't look at Silly here."

"Silly?"

"My dog's name is Sylvia but I call her Silly."

The little poodle's head popped up at the sound of her name.

"What caught your attention?" Claire asked.

"He was a very fit young man, with sunglasses that had mirrors. He also had a neatly trimmed beard. That's important to me. I don't like the beards these men have where it's all unshaven and halfway down their neck. A neatly trimmed beard is a sign of class and very distinguished."

"I see."

"He had a backpack with him and I wondered if he was homeless, but then I figured not because of the nice beard. Oh, and he had a weird tattoo."

Clair raised an eyebrow.

"Tattoo?"

"Yes, when he reached his backpack after I tried to talk to him, his arm caught my cyc and there was a big scary thing on his arm. It was a horrible thing. It looked like a skull with flames and a gun. The whole thing scared me and I think Silly was scared, too. She growled which she never does and then she whimpered. I realized he was no nice young man. Probably a bad person. That's what made me remember him when you asked."

Claire thanked the old lady and Silly, got her information and spent two more hours asking questions but no one provided anything new. She headed back toward the station.

All she had was a tattoo.

But it was better than nothing.

CHAPTER EIGHT

The custom seaplane floating in the turquoise blue waters just off the Bahamian mainland sported the name *Peregrine*. It was a vintage Boeing aircraft made for the Navy in the 1930s and had since been completely overhauled.

Instead of a utilitarian vessel devoid of personality, it had now been turned into a luxury hotel suite that could go airborne. It featured three spacious cabins, two bathrooms, an office and a complete host of electronics, including satellite communications enabling high-speed internet and cellular networks.

The plane's owner was also the pilot; a former pilot and member of the Special Forces.

He was a rugged man, broad in both shoulders

and chest, with a narrow waist and powerful legs. His hair was close-cropped and the color of gunmetal. His nose was flattened, and his teeth were straight and even, but dull in color as if tempered by years of whiskey and cigarettes.

The man, known by his online friends as Follett, was reading the crime report of an old man who'd been gunned down in New York City. Shot from long distance by a sniper, was the current hypothesis.

Follett sank into one of the leather club chairs that gave him a vantage point view of the water outside. The plane had a row of windows, the one through which he now looked was the biggest of them. It was his favorite spot in the aircraft, other than the bedroom.

The water was gorgeous, like topaz and as smooth as glass. In the distance, not even a wave rippled.

Usually, the sight of the water made him relaxed and peaceful, but the news was unsettling. He knew the man who'd been murdered. Knew him quite well, and the role he played in a certain organization.

Follett no longer felt calm.

He was triggered by the news article and he needed to take action. Anger was a form of arousal and he remembered with relish what he had in the bedroom.

For now, he pushed that idea aside.

This was bad news, there was no way around it; no way to spin it as some kind of opportunity, which is what Follett normally tried to do in dire circumstances. It's what he'd been trained to do.

Visually, he kept seeing the man he knew being shot in the head. Follett had seen long-distance head shots made by snipers under his command. He'd seen a great deal of them. He knew what hey looked like, what they even sounded like. How the victim's body crumpled after impact, half of the head blown to smithereens.

The dead man hadn't really been his friend, per se, more of a business associate.

They were partners, in a sense.

Follett heaved himself to his feet and walked into the bedroom.

On the bed was a very young man. His wrists and ankles were bound.

The youth looked up at him with fear.

Follett stripped off his shirt and dropped his swim trunks to reveal his highly excited manhood.

"I'll make them pay, eventually," he said. "But you'll do for now."

With nothing but empty ocean for miles around the seaplane, no one could hear the young man scream.

CHAPTER NINE

Congressman Hector Ortiz had provided his constituency with a major surprise long before the second occurred.

Nearly ten years earlier, he'd run as a huge underdog going against an established opponent who'd spent nearly twenty years in office. No one had given Ortiz a shot. His ideas were too controversial, his experience too profound, his skin color too dark.

But he'd pulled it off and become one of the youngest congressmen to ever take office.

That had been a long time ago and now, he pulled off a second surprise. He had just triumphantly submitted a bill to the house floor that would set new goals for clean energy, protection of the environment and voters' rights. It was, he positioned, a revolutionary moment. Everything would change, he told the young people. They cheered.

But Ortiz thought they were ignorant.

The bill didn't stand much chance of passing, but that wasn't the point; things were never as they seemed in Washington. Simply getting a bill to the floor, beginning dialogue and, more importantly, for Ortiz to say he'd gotten the legislation thus far was a victory in and of itself.

A political victory, even if nothing much good would come of it. Of course, in Ortiz's eyes, getting himself reelected for yet another term was a very good thing, indeed.

A lifelong bachelor, Congressman Ortiz had his assistant book him a table for four at his favorite eatery: a gourmet DC restaurant called *Selva* that was his standby favorite after any kind of success.

His guests would all be friends, none of whom would accompany him back to his penthouse bachelor pad not far from the Capitol.

Ortiz sat in the back of the black SUV with tinted, bulletproof windows.

He sipped from a glass of scotch as the big vehicle maneuvered its way to the restaurant. Tonight would be a very good night, a celebration of his latest and greatest accomplishment.

He would enjoy more scotch, a glass of wine, a great meal, lively conversation, and cap it off with a night of playtime back in his big bed.

The congressman was almost tempted to access some of his favorite images on his cell phone, but decided against it. One, he tried not to look at them at all. And second, even though it was his personal phone, not the one supplied by the taxpayer dollars, it was meant to be done carefully and selectively.

Besides, they were almost to *Selva*.

Ortiz drained the rest of his drink and waited for his driver to open the door. He could see through the darkened window that the doorman was already opening the restaurant door and he could imagine his favorite table; in the back, with a great view of anyone who came into the place. Waited on by not one, but two waiters who made sure to never leave anyone at Ortiz's table wanting.

The congressman stepped onto the pavement and heard the door to the SUV bang shut behind him.

The second bang was one Ortiz never heard.

Because before the sound arrived, the bullet that blew apart the congressman's head reached its target.

CHAPTER TEN

Killing gets easier.

Someone told him that when he was first starting out and he'd hoped, at the time, that it wasn't true. He didn't want to be one of those guys who could bestow death upon another human being with utter detachment. Where killing someone was as mundane as taking out the garbage or flushing the toilet.

But the advice turned out to be absolutely correct.

And it became a truism much sooner than he would have liked.

It was almost as if the first man he'd killed, an enemy combatant, was the first and only time he'd contemplated what he'd done. After that, they had all just been more deaths. He still remembered that first kill. The rest of them?

Not at all.

He knew that he'd ended their lives with the pull of a trigger. All at long distance. From the end of his rifle.

But it was different now.

In a sense, the old man at the dog park and now the congressman were enemy combatants. Unarmed, of course. But they'd been waging their own kind of war for many years and now, both karma and a bullet had finally arrived. It had been fired a long time ago and had taken its time reaching the target, but that it did.

This one had definitely been trickier, what with the secret service in tow. So he'd taken some extra precautions. Backed out even further than usual which gave him plenty of time to pack up his weapon, descend to his rental car and disappear from the area before anyone even knew where to look.

For now, Rider was pleased with his progress.

He glanced over at the passenger seat, looked at the pack with his rifle.

Just the two of us once again, he thought.

His burner cell phone rang and he glanced at the screen, and remembered that he was wrong.

CHAPTER ELEVEN

Michael Tallon was careful not to skyline himself. Meaning, rather than run over the crest of a hill, he tried to run alongside it and wait for an opening that didn't bring him out on top of the rise and make him visible for miles on end.

It was an old habit and probably not necessary in his backyard – which was the ever empty expanse of Death Valley.

Still, today was different.

Because he was being followed.

There were no if, ands or buts about it; there was a superstition among men like Tallon that the feeling of being watched was real. Mountain men used to claim they had the ability, yet Tallon believed it to be true only because he believed in subconscious clues.

The image of something in one's peripheral vision that didn't necessarily register. A sound or a shadow felt, but not noticed on a conscious level.

These things could add up.

He was on the last mile of his run, heading back toward his ranch, when the feeling came to him. He'd stopped twice and pretended to adjust his shoe or catch his breath, peering behind him for any glimpse of something out of place. A shadow where it shouldn't belong, a shape that seemed wrong.

But there was nothing but desert rock and cactus and dust.

Now, he sprinted down a short incline and took one last look back over his shoulder, but this time while he was on the move.

The tactic worked.

Tallon finally saw his pursuer.

It was a mountain lion, less than a hundred yards away.

Tallon knew they didn't hunt humans as a normal course of business; they only targeted people when they were usually sick or starving or both. This one looked thin and Tallon considered letting the cat get close and then shooting him.

Instead, he jogged back to his ranch, all the time with his hand on the pistol at the back of his running shorts.

The cat was either too weak or lacked the desperation to actually attack.

Tallon reached the back of his ranch house – a modest adobe structure – and let himself in.

He retrieved his binoculars and studied the cat who had stopped, probably getting the scents of various human activities and dealing with alarm bells. Tallon could get a rifle and drop the cat now.

Instead, he watched and soon the mountain lion disappeared back into the foothills that were now burning red with the setting sun.

Tallon put his binoculars back, stripped off his sweat-drenched clothes and showered. Just as he was getting dressed, his cell phone buzzed with a text.

He glanced at the screen.

It was from one of his former special ops buddies and the message was simple:

Remember that dude who shot RKN74?

Tallon did, in fact, remember the man. Or, at least, he remembered the stories about him.

A second text popped up.

Think this was him?

Before Tallon could answer either message, a web link popped up.

It was to a news article.

Tallon read the headline: ***Elderly Brooklyn Man Shot by Sniper.***

CHAPTER TWELVE

Dissecting a man's history was no easy task. Detective Claire Brewster didn't assume it would be, yet she was surprised at the degree of difficulty in getting past Victor Panko's most recent activities.

She read through what she had so far: Victor Panko was sixty-eight years old, single, with no children. He ran a charity that raised funds for an international humanitarian organization.

Claire studied the documents before her and knew it wouldn't suffice.

He had a history and it seemed New York had been his home for all of his life. But the information was surprisingly sparse.

She forwarded a request for more information on the charity itself, including names, addresses and company filings with a specialist at the NYPD who tracked down financial information. In the meantime, Claire would also do some snooping around.

Just as she was set to take the search warrant she had for Panko's apartment, an email popped up on her computer with a red flag attached.

She clicked on it and read about the assassination of a congressman in D.C.

Claire frowned – none of her cases had any political involvement.

She scrolled through the email, looking for the text that would be highlighted to indicate why she was flagged.

And then, near the end of the information, she saw the words:

RKN74.

CHAPTER THIRTEEN

Jack Reacher's unit had been the Army's 110th MP. All paperwork, case histories, files and personnel records would be stored digitally within the firewalls of the Pentagon.

Pauling herself had no way to access them. She'd maintained access to some of the FBI's system thanks to a few loopholes exploited by a former client of hers whose specialty was breaching firewalls. It helped that Pauling had been an employee of the FBI and it had been more of a matter of keeping access, as opposed to obtaining it illegally.

The Pentagon, however, was a whole different ball game.

For that, she used a former client who'd been

wrongfully terminated by his employer. That employer, a large multinational bank, had employed him as a hacker. However, when he'd uncovered a few shenanigans being employed by the bank's upper management team, he'd been fired, and framed for embezzling.

Pauling not only helped clear his name but she also earned him tens of millions of dollars in an out-of-court settlement.

Now he worked as a private consultant, and did any jobs for which Pauling sought his assistance. She reached out to him and asked him to dig around for anything in Jack Reacher's official Army files, or his unit's files, that tied to activity in Afghanistan. Activity that might somehow be construed as criminal.

That done, she began to investigate what she could: war crimes committed by the Army in Afghanistan. Her decision to focus solely on the Army was a bit of a risk; she knew that. The fact of the matter was more and more teams in the military, especially special ops, were a mixture of different branches. Delta brushed shoulders with SEAL teams. Green Berets might have a Navy comms officer in their team.

Hell, there were even international teams where Americans might have a Canadian or

Australian as part of the group. The British Special Air Service were legendary, and sometimes might rub shoulders with Americans.

So technically, a war crime could be committed by every branch of the military, even if their mission wasn't solely their responsibility.

But there was no way she could investigate them all. Not that there were hundreds of war crimes, but things were often handled internally and to snoop through the Army, Air Force, Marines, Navy and National Guard files would have been too much. It would be thousands and thousands of incidents, files and reports that would take a dozen investigators working around the clock.

She had no choice but to focus only on one branch.

Besides, Jack Reacher had been Army and to her knowledge, MPs weren't often included as part of a multi-branch team. They tended to work alone.

What gave her some hope was that for an incident to be elevated to the status of war crime, it had to be something out of the ordinary. Not a case of friendly fire, or a questionable military action.

Additionally, as Reacher was being flagged as a

war criminal, the first organization to look at would be the Army. If nothing came of it, maybe she would widen her net, but she didn't think that was going to be the case.

Pauling began with public databases, including news organizations and LexisNexis, using search terms *war crimes, Afghanistan, criminal, murder*, etc.

What came back was fairly minimal, a fact that surprised Pauling.

There had been a massacre of an Afghani family by a psychopath and his team. The retaliation had been just as bad: an entire squad had been wiped out by local Afghanis. The investigation had been above board and conclusive, thoroughly covered with all perpetrators known and accounted for.

There was no mention of Reacher.

Sexual assaults had been plentiful; but again, nothing major and no sign of a wider conspiracy.

No, to be labeled a war crime, Pauling reasoned, it would have to be something especially heinous.

And that meant it would almost certainly be newsworthy – if the information was ever made public.

And so far, she'd found nothing.

Pauling closed down her computer and paced her loft apartment.

She decided to retrieve her new pal: the Colt Peacemaker, and head to the range. Shooting at targets helped her think.

Maybe as she was blowing away imaginary bad guys, she might think of a way to catch a real one.

CHAPTER FOURTEEN

Follett dumped the body of the young man at sea. He felt nothing as he watched the adolescent sink down to the bottom of the Atlantic, wrapped in chains.

From his vantage point on the deck of the seaplane *Peregrine*, Follett knew no one would find anything as he wasn't far from the Gulf Stream, the warm current of water that accounted for so much life in the ocean. The scent of the youth's blood and rotting flesh would draw carnivores from all depths of the waters and within days if not hours, nothing would be left.

Follett secured all of the doors and windows on the plane, making sure there was no trace of the youth's existence on board. He would do a second, even more thorough sterilization of the interior when he landed back in the US. Or, more accurately, his staff would see to it.

The big engines of the plane came to life and soon he was lifting off from the water. He'd spent a small fortune refurbishing the plane. It had come into this world decades ago mostly as first a military transport plane and then a few years later as a commercial cargo hauler before it was listed for sale.

It sat for years garnering little interest and Follett was able to acquire it for far below the asking price. He spent millions upgrading all aspects of the plane, both mechanical and aesthetic, to make it worthy of a private jet. But he liked the anonymity of the ocean, being able to land anywhere he wanted.

Now, he headed for his private hangar at a marina just outside New York City. He had a mansion not far from where he kept the plane. In less than two hours, he was pulling his Bentley convertible into the garage beneath the Long Island home.

An elevator brought him to the top floor of the three-story mansion and he showered, shaved, and changed into his typical daily uniform: linen slacks, leather sandals, and a heavy cotton shirt.

He grabbed a heavy leaded crystal glass from

the kitchen and splashed some aged whiskey into it and then went to his office. Follett logged onto the computer and waited for the others to arrive.

It didn't take long.

They appeared as video thumbnails on his screen and the audio bogged down with their panic. They were all trying to speak at once and because of the different browser speeds, the result was a garbled mess.

Follett held up his hand and after a few moments everyone became silent.

He already knew they were losing their minds over their partner's death in Brooklyn. There's nothing more permanent than getting one's head blown off and Follett didn't blame them for their fear. But it's what one does with their fear that defines a man.

Once they'd all fallen silent, Follett took command, without the need to rehash what everyone already knew.

"Here's what we're going to do," he began.

CHAPTER FIFTEEN

In the field, a sniper has a spotter. The spotter's job is to help identify targets, judge wind, angle and other factors, and also help the shooter make adjustments in the event a target is missed.

For Rider, he'd worked with a spotter when he was in the military. Once he'd moved on to private work, he'd started working alone and had come to prefer it.

It made sense because the one time he almost died, the closest he'd ever come to cashing in his chips for good, was when his spotter betrayed him.

It had happened in Afghanistan, after he'd alerted his superior office to a problem within the unit. They'd gone out to an area activity north of their base. Something had felt off to Rider, but he hadn't been able to put a finger on it.

When he was in position, his spotter had fallen back slightly.

After a period of time, Rider had gotten into "the zone" and time was relative, he'd realized his spotter hadn't said a word, hadn't recommended adjustments.

Rider looked back.

His spotter was gone.

That's when he heard the bombs falling.

The first impact was so close it felt like his body had been torn apart, but he was still conscious. The second bomb hit, and he didn't remember anything after that.

When he finally came to, he was fighting for his life, surrounded by strangers.

But he survived.

Barely.

With no help from his spotter.

So now, he was working alone and it was as natural to him as anything. However, he wasn't really a solo operation. He had a spotter, in a sense, just not in the field.

Her name was Reese and the incoming call on his burner phone was her number.

"Hey," he said.

"Change of plans," she said.

Rider's hand steadied on the wheel. He didn't like sudden changes as they almost always led to mistakes. And mistakes in his line of work were the kind that meant you never made another one.

"We've got an opportunity back in New York too good to pass up," Reese continued. "It's one we've been waiting for."

"As long as it's not too good to be true," Rider replied.

He heard Reese laugh softly on the other end of the line.

"My job is to identify the targets," she said. "Have I ever steered you wrong?"

"No," Rider said.

But in his mind, he was thinking, *not yet*.

CHAPTER SIXTEEN

Tallon read the text message from his buddy, Brock, about the murder in Brooklyn.

Rather than responding with a text of his own, he called him directly. Secretly, Tallon hated texting and always preferred actual conversation. Especially when it came to something like this.

"What the hell are you up to, Brock?" Tallon asked.

In the background, Tallon thought he could hear a baseball game announcer.

"Just watching the Tigers lose again," Brock said. He was a lifelong Detroiter and always wore a Detroit Tigers baseball cap. Tallon knew Brock could cite statistics for every Tigers team going all the way back to the days of Ty Cobb.

Suddenly, the sound of the baseball game stopped.

"What about you?" Brock asked.

"Just got back from a run."

"Same old Tallon."

Tallon sat back in his leather club chair in the living room and put his feet up on the matching ottoman. It was true; his commitment to fitness had been a bit legendary even among Special Forces. Still, he wasn't that young anymore and he would feel the effects of the run in about a half hour or so. It was the kind of soreness he welcomed.

"So you got my message?" Brock asked.

"Sure did. So how do you know it was an RKN74?"

Brock sighed. "I can't name names but a buddy of mine from Detroit works for NYPD's SWAT team. Apparently, they were talking about this old guy getting nailed by a sniper right there in the middle of Brooklyn. And then the ballistics that came in were super weird – and he remembered me telling him about that guy we both sort of knew of."

Tallon smiled inwardly at Brock's reticence to be specific. But he knew exactly what he was talking about. When they'd both been deployed in Afghanistan, they'd heard about a legendary sniper who insisted on using a certain kind of Russian ammunition.

That, in and of itself, wasn't unusual.

What was unusual were the rumors about the sniper himself. People said he was like a ghost and there was speculation he did a lot of work off the books. The kind of work no one wanted to talk about.

"I thought he was dead," Tallon said.

He hadn't thought about the shooter in years because of that: word had spread that the sniper had been killed behind enemy lines on one of those "non-sanctioned" missions. It was the kind of story that often occurred among men like them; lies and whispers were the cornerstone of their occupation. Sometimes, stories just took on lives of their own.

"Maybe he was," Brock replied. His voice betrayed a certain lack of confidence in the statement.

"From what little we know about the guy, this would be right up his alley," Tallon said. Meaning, the guy was mysterious to begin with, a dispute over whether he was actually dead or not would make perfect sense.

"But why an old man in Brooklyn?"

"Maybe it was his ammo, but not him."

Brock scoffed. "Seems strange: a legendary sniper and his custom ammunition are used by another sniper? The guy was a ghost, remember? It's not like he had a bunch of buddies he shared his information with."

Tallon realized he'd forgotten the man's nickname.

"That's right – everyone called him the Ghost," Tallon said.

"Not quite. Ghost Rider was the full handle. But most people shortened it."

"Oh yeah," Tallon said. "Rider."

CHAPTER SEVENTEEN

"She took the bait," Foley said.

He was thin with a ferret-like face, dressed all in black: black nylon parachute pants, black t-shirt and black boots.

Behind him towered a second man dressed all in black.

"About time," the bigger man said.

They both watched a computer terminal with a direct access portal into the Pentagon's system. It was an authorized access. The computer station was in the middle of the room, facing floor-to-ceiling glass windows that gave them a view of the bucolic Virginia countryside. Even though it wasn't visible from this vantage point, the office was located less than five miles from the headquarters of the Central Intelligence Agency.

The big man's name was Jekell. No one knew if that was his real name or a nickname derived from the infamous Jekyll and Hyde story. Most thought it was his real name because the big man did not have any kind of split personality: he was characterized by one overpowering personality characteristic: he lived to destroy.

"Are you sure we need her?" Foley asked, without taking his eyes from the computer screen. His thin, sallow face took on a slightly blue hue from the glow of the screen. It made his pencil-thin moustache look like a digital shadow. "I mean, the NYPD is after him, and now the FBI, too, since he whacked Ortiz. You don't kill a congressman and get away with it."

Jekell's face remained impassive. "You should think before you speak. I don't really care if he gets caught. I care about what he can say if he does. We can't let that happen. It's more important than ever we find him first. So yes, we sure as hell need her."

"Tell me as soon as she takes action, and keep me updated on the Feebies," Jekell ordered.

"Sure," Foley said. "Where will you be if I need to get ahold of you fast?"

The door slammed shut with Jekell's response.

"Okay, then," Foley said to the empty room.

CHAPTER EIGHTEEN

"I've got good news and I've got bad news," Pauling's hacker said over a secure line. It actually wasn't a cell phone – it was a private chat room the hacker, whose name was a rather mundane Dave, had set up. He told Pauling it was the safest way for them to communicate. Rather than relying on a cellular carrier and network, he was in complete control of the feed. Security, he said, was airtight.

"Start with the bad," Pauling said. She was in the safety of her loft but still felt the need to be clandestine.

"Okay."

She studied his small thumbnail video image on her computer screen. He looked exactly like what he was: a middle-aged man who spent most of his time sitting at a desk. He had sandy hair tinged with gray and a plain shirt with a collar. Dave would not have done well in prison, and they both knew it. That might have had something to do with his undying commitment to Pauling.

"The bad news is my visit into the Pentagon's computers did not go unnoticed," he said.

Pauling didn't like the sound of that. It was a pretty serious offense that could result in serious time for both of them. But Dave was the best at what he did and she had a feeling he was about to explain why she shouldn't be worried.

"Here's why you shouldn't be worried," Dave said, on cue. "They know I went in, but they don't know who or where I am. If they were to actually trace my access – it would lead them to a computer in Iceland which was just smashed into pieces and dumped into a glacial lake, thanks to an associate who has no idea who or where I am. It's amazing what you can buy on the Internet."

"Okay, that's better," Pauling said. "The good news?"

"The good news is, I think I found what you were looking for."

A new desktop folder icon appeared miraculously on Pauling's computer screen.

"I literally ran a million different searches with all the variables you mentioned and this is the only thing that came up," Dave said. "When I read it, it seems like the thing you might be looking for. And since it was literally the only single thing I could find, I'm hoping I'm right."

"Okay, thank you, Dave. Let me know how much I owe you." Even though he would have done the work for free, Pauling insisted on paying even though it wasn't on her official books.

A document appeared on Pauling's screen and she knew it was Dave's bill.

"You got it, Pauling. Let me know if you need any more help."

Dave's video image went away and Pauling double-clicked on the folder.

It contained a single document with the heading *Criminal Investigation Command*. Pauling noted the date and the absence of names. The page contained only two paragraphs:

"110th MP seeking information regarding multiple homicides and civilian abductions north of Mehtar Lam."

. . .

Pauling knew FOB stood for Forward Operating Base. Mehtar Lam was certainly a city or region in Afghanistan.

The last paragraph was what had most likely been flagged by Dave's search parameters within the Pentagon's files:

"Seeking information on rogue unit named Grim Reaper as reported by multiple intel sources. Recommend immediate full investigation and full resource allocation. Also recommend highest classification for secured communication."

Pauling read through the paragraphs twice and then looked again at the date.

Knowing Reacher's history, the date was right around the time of his dismissal from the Army.

Had his departure from the military been because of this investigation? Had it triggered his leaving the Army? Or was it merely coincidence?

Pauling didn't believe in luck or bad timing. Things usually happened for a reason.

Now she sat back and pondered the term Grim Reaper. Could someone have labeled Reacher that? Had he killed multiple civilians and then been ejected from the Army and now someone had dug up evidence of the crime?

No way. Not Jack Reacher.

It was something else.

It had to be.

She already knew investigating a multiple homicide in Afghanistan by a rogue unit was going to be next to impossible. Even though now she had more information. She would have to find out where the hell Mehtar Lam was.

And then double-check and see if Reacher had ever spent time there, although she was positive he hadn't: she'd read his file so often that she practically had it memorized. As far as she could tell he'd never been stationed, or worked in, Afghanistan.

This was all she had so far.

Where next?

At first she was at a loss but then like all good answers, the solution was simple. How had she heard of Reacher's link to a crime in the first place? It wasn't through the Army or the CIA.

It had been via her old pal Haskins at the FBI.

Maybe now that Pauling had a location of the crime, Mehtar Lam, she could use Haskins to work the Bureau for any active or former homicide cases. Typically, the CIA handled investigations internationally, but sometimes the lines were blurred and it was Haskins who'd delivered the news in the first place.

Pauling sent her friend a message and a suggestion they meet for a drink, if possible. She also asked, ever heard of Mehtar Lam?

Minutes later, Haskins agreed to the drink, but didn't answer her question.

That was okay, Pauling wasn't looking for a response.

It had been a subtle hint for Haskins to look into that location and bring anything she could find to their next meeting.

Pauling hoped her friend had gotten the message.

CHAPTER NINETEEN

The older black man walked from his living room to the kitchen and then stopped in the hallway.

He was out of breath.

At his age, despite the commitment to staying healthy, cardio wasn't his strong suit.

His name was Barnes and he was just under six feet tall. He wore jeans, a Nike dri-fit T-shirt and slippers. His hair was tightly cropped and tinged with silver. His home, a third floor apartment in Queens was the epitome of a man cave: everything was utilitarian and devoid of any feminine touches. Most of the decorations were sports posters. In the living room, homemade shelves carried the burden of thirty-year-old football trophies. Division II.

Barnes had a touch of asthma. His lungs were making a strange sound, sort of like a slow squeak that would disappear and reappear without any kind of rhythm, like a balloon with a slow leak.

It was this goddamned stupid thing he was doing.

He had to keep moving. Sit in the living room, take a seat and then get up again. Hold his cell phone to his ear, even though there was no one on the end of the line. Walk into the kitchen. Turn on the lights. Sit at the table. Go to the fridge, grab a beer.

Go back to the living room.

Ridiculous. His knees hurt and now his back hurt, too. Besides, every time he grabbed a beer he drank and now he had to piss again. He was going to be drunker than a skunk by the time this was all over.

Climb the stairs to his bedroom. Turn on a light. Then turn off the light and go back to the living room.

It was good exercise, but the thing was, he didn't need to exercise. He had prostate cancer and his doctor had told him he would be dead within the year. It was a horrible way to die because he could no longer have sex and for him, that was the only thing he really lived for anymore. Take that away, and he was just a sack of meat holding up some middle-of-the-road clothing, stinking up an apartment he'd paid off years ago.

Still, this was giving him at least some entertainment.

He knew what was going on.

And if it worked, it would be worth the effort.

If it didn't, well, *what the hell did he have to lose?*

CHAPTER TWENTY

Rider was patient. In fact, he doubted there was another person within one hundred square miles who had the sort of self-discipline and willingness to remain still and focused that he possessed.

Having said that, he was slightly annoyed.

Reese had given him the target's information and he'd scouted the location, choosing the rooftop less than a thousand feet away as the ideal spot. It was almost like the location had been perfectly chosen for a sniper.

The location was the easy part.

The problem was the target.

The older black man was staying maddeningly mobile, and seemed to prefer sitting locations that left him behind a wall or pillar through which Rider couldn't shoot.

It was almost like the man was playing peek-a-boo with him.

As Rider waited for the shot, he moved several times, looking for a better vantage point. Each time he modified his own location, he knew it made him vulnerable. It was a bad strategy for a sniper. It was better to lock in and be still, rather than moving around. To be mobile was infantry. He wasn't infantry, he was an assassin.

He thought about what he'd said to Reese: *don't steer me wrong*.

Reese was the best spotter he'd ever had.

When he'd come back in Afghanistan after having been betrayed by his spotter, he'd been taken in by a family. They'd lost one of their sons to the very people Rider had reported. The boy who disappeared had an older sister; her name was Reshawna and in his opium-fueled delirium he'd started calling her Reese. Not only had she nursed him, but she helped smuggle him out of Afghanistan, and later, he'd returned the favor. Together, they'd taken on a shared mission.

He knew she would never betray him.

But something about this target didn't feel right.

His nerves remained calm but his sniper's sixth sense was alive and well.

The damned old black man had just gotten up from his chair and moved once again to the spot in the kitchen hidden in the corner.

Rider took the moment to pull his eye back from the rifle scope.

As he did, he caught the slightest bit of movement to his left.

He glanced over the rooftops, sure it was a flutter of clothes from a clothesline some penny pincher had set up to dry clothes. Electricity on a dryer cost money, after all. Let the wind do the work, and pocket the difference.

Rider looked at the clothesline, but it was still. There was virtually no breeze.

His eyes focused just beyond the clothesline to the next roof, where he saw the top of something. It looked like—

Rider dove just as he saw the silhouette across the rooftops jolt with the kick of a rifle.

Something tore into Rider's left forearm as he rolled onto the asphalt roof.

He had dragged his rifle with him and now, he came to a squat with the rifle held tightly against his right shoulder.

The pain in his arm wasn't bad, even as blood poured from the wound.

He crabbed across the roof to the far corner, making calculations in his mind. He'd already factored various distances and knew that his rifle was set up for about the right distance. The only question was, could he bring his rifle up and get off the shot?

Only one way to find out: he rose in a fluid motion and found the spot just beyond the clothesline.

It was empty.

Time to go, Rider thought as he raced for the stairwell.

CHAPTER TWENTY-ONE

"Shit!" Follett shouted at the computer screen.

He had landed Peregrine and handed it over to his team at the marina. Now, he was in his home office, staring at a computer screen. He still wore his linen slacks, sandals and cotton shirt but all that was forgotten as he roared at the video playing before him.

The sniper on the roof across from Rider had clearly missed. The GoPro camera mounted on the man's head had given Follett a beautiful view of the whole thing. The camera had live streamed the action straight back to Follett so he could watch his old friend Rider die a most poetic death: shot in the head by a sniper.

Follett and his team had so perfectly set up

the old black man as a decoy, told him to keep moving back and forth, to not give anyone a clear shot.

In the meantime, they'd positioned their own shooter three buildings away, strategically positioned to focus on the only vantage point a qualified sniper would utilize.

And now, their shooter had missed.

Follett got to his feet.

He went to his gun safe and made a selection.

Then, he went to another bedroom – the mansion had no fewer than eight of them.

He opened the door and smiled at the Afghani woman tied to the chair. She was beautiful, even though she had a gag in her mouth and her face was badly bruised. Follett was not aroused by any of it.

It had taken a lot of work to find her, and a lot of money in bribes, but it had worked. The problem was, finding her was always going to be much easier than finding Rider.

"Oh, Reese," Follett said to the woman. "This just isn't your lucky day."

CHAPTER TWENTY-TWO

Rider flew down the stairs, his boots clanging on the metal. He had his rifle slung across his shoulder and a 9mm pistol in his right hand.

The bullet had simply seared his left forearm. No real damage had been done. He'd been lucky.

Very lucky.

Now, he burst through the door into the alley behind the building and raced around the corner. His rental car was parked in a spot in front of a deli and he'd probably gone over the meter, waiting for his shot. That was bad form; a parking ticket was proof that you had been at a certain place at a certain point of time.

As he ran, he knew all along he'd been set up.

Compromised.

The black man had purposely kept moving to keep him waiting for the shot, all while they'd set up their own.

Damnit, he thought.

He had to get word to Reese.

If he was blown, she was too.

He saw his car ahead just as shots rang out and bullets clipped the brickwork next to his head. Bits of broken stone tore into his face and he saw the shooter on his left. The man had probably descended from the rooftop where he'd taken his shot at Rider.

The timing made sense.

Anger burned inside Rider and he was determined to make it out of the mission alive.

Rider fired as he ran and the man ducked down. Rider made it to his car, threw his rifle inside and saw another blur of movement in his peripheral vision.

The man had ducked around a parked car and was aiming a pistol at Rider.

Rider did the opposite of what the man expected: rather than slide further into the car in order to start it and escape, he sprang outward, away from the steering wheel.

It was classic sniper strategy: put yourself where they won't expect you.

The man's shot blew apart the side view mirror, missing Rider by at least two feet.

Rider aimed carefully and fired twice, a double tap, and saw his bullets blow apart the man's head. The body fell to the curb, slack.

It wasn't the most elegant kill, but definitely one of the more satisfying, Rider thought.

He was tempted to run across and look for identification on the dead man but it didn't matter. He knew who they were. Rider needed to get the hell out of there; sirens were already getting louder and he had to call Reese.

Assuming she was still alive.

Behind the wheel, he threw the car into gear and drove fast, putting ten city blocks behind him before he fished out his cell phone.

He dialed Reese and waited, his breath slowly going back to normal.

On the third ring, his call was answered.

"Hello Rider," a voice said. "Reese can't come to the phone right now because...she's dead."

Rider listened to the man laugh and he recognized Follett's voice.

"You're a dead man walking," Rider said.

He disconnected the call and broke the phone into pieces, tossing them out of the car as he drove.

CHAPTER TWENTY-THREE

Tallon studied the mountain lion through his spotting scope. He could see the big cat was starving; his ribs were visible and he looked gaunt.

Tallon brought the rifle to his shoulder, aimed, and fired.

The cat flopped onto its side.

Even for Death Valley it was hot; over one hundred degrees and not an ounce of breeze. It was late afternoon, the sun was still high overhead and even the birds were somewhere in the shade. The sky was nothing but pure blue, designed to make the heat as intense as possible.

Tallon jogged ahead and studied the fallen animal. He was still breathing. Tallon had fired a tranquilizer and now, the cat was knocked out.

Tallon could see the mountain lion's broken leg. It was infected. Tallon traced a line of green all the way from the break into the big predator's chest. No wonder the mountain lion had followed him; he was dying, and he probably knew it.

There was no chance he could take the cat back to a vet in his little town; the infection would be too far gone. Froth on the cat's mouth was the telltale sign.

With a heavy heart, Tallon placed the muzzle of his pistol against the cat's head and fired.

It was the only way.

He walked back to his ranch and cleaned the pistol. His cell phone vibrated and he checked the screen.

It was his buddy Brock.

This time the message was a bit longer.

Ever hear of Jack Reacher? He has something to do with our buddy.

Tallon frowned.

Reacher?

The name didn't mean much to him, but Pauling had told him about the dude: an Army MP who kicked ass everywhere he went. Tallon's kind of guy.

What did Reacher have to do with the sniper he and Brock knew from Afghanistan?

Tallon hit the "Favorites" button on his phone and saw Pauling's number.

He tapped it.

He was going to call her anyway, now he had a question for her.

CHAPTER TWENTY-FOUR

Detective Claire Brewster whistled at the contents of Victor Panko's computer. The tech guys had finally broken through the complicated encryption on the old man's desktop.

For a man who worked for a charity, he was big on secrecy.

The team had found a cache of child pornography: thousands of images and videos that made Claire sick to her stomach.

The charity, she found out, was supposedly an orphanage in Afghanistan.

But what Claire and her team soon discovered was that the orphanage didn't exist. There was no physical structure – they'd used aerial photography and images from the military to scour the area.

There was nothing but a small village, ravaged by war and the opium trade.

Clearly, the orphanage was really just a pipeline of young children from a war-torn country delivered directly to pedophiles.

Mostly in the US.

Claire had read the names with great interest. They were listed as individuals who'd filed for "adoption." In most cases, the names were fake as were the phone numbers and addresses. But a member of the team had discovered the cypher and broken down the code.

Real names and real numbers had appeared before them.

One of the list of Americans welcoming young, pre-adolescent boys into the US: the recently deceased Congressman Ortiz.

Claire realized she was in the middle of something much bigger than she'd first thought.

A ring of pedophiles.

Which was certainly a crime in and of itself.

More interesting, however, was the ensuing crime that had brought the ring to her attention in the first place.

Someone was killing them.

One shot at a time.

CHAPTER TWENTY-FIVE

The bar was called the Double Olive and it was a martini bar in central Manhattan. Pauling arrived first and ordered a dirty martini with a blue cheese stuffed olive. It was clearly the after-work crowd: lots of ties loosened, voices getting progressively louder and corporate angst being relieved.

It was a ritual Pauling had experienced firsthand.

A man on the other end of the bar was getting ready to approach Pauling. He'd been making obvious eye contact, and had chugged his last drink for courage, when, thankfully, Haskins arrived.

She slid onto the stool next to Pauling and they gave each other a quick hug.

Pauling was surprised to smell the scent of alcohol on Haskins.

Had she stopped somewhere else first?

Haskins ordered a dry martini and when it came they clinked glasses.

"So much better than espresso," Pauling joked.

"I can't argue with that," Haskins replied.

"How was work?" Pauling asked, wondering if her friend was slurring her words slightly. If so, that was a very bad sign.

"Busy, busy, busy," Haskins said. "This Russian oligarch is into all kinds of shit. How about you?"

"I'm tied up on this Reacher thing," Pauling said. For the time being, she wasn't going to confront Haskins on what was potentially an issue. "Turns out, there was an investigation in Afghanistan, but I don't think Reacher was involved because it was just after he'd left the Army. Still, this whole notion of a unit called the Grim Reaper seems over the top, even for war time. Were you able to find out anything?"

Haskins looked aside.

"What's wrong?" Pauling asked.

Her friend's hand shook as she picked up her martini.

"I'm going to tell you something but you have

to swear you won't tell anyone else. I'll deny it to my dying breath."

"Okay," Pauling said. She studied her friend: her eyes were wide and slightly bloodshot.

"I've got a problem," Haskins said. "And someone knows about it, and they asked me to mention the Reacher thing to you. And they also said if you asked about this case, I was supposed to give you this."

Haskins withdrew an envelope from her soft leather briefcase, folded in half.

"It's the investigation you were asking about," Haskins said. "I don't know if it's true or not, but it has to do with an Army officer named Brad Follett. A bad guy. And...and, I've got a problem but my friendship with you is more important."

Haskins was about to start crying and Pauling wanted to comfort her friend.

"But why?"

"I don't know. All I know is I looked up this Follett guy and he's a dangerous man. You need to be careful."

Haskins drank the rest of her martini in one gulp.

"I've got to go," she said.

"No," Pauling said. "Let me–"

"If I say anything else I'll be in trouble."

She put a hand on Pauling's wrist. The hand was ice cold.

"I'm sorry, Lauren. I need help. But not now."

Haskins left and Pauling watched her go, as guilt consumed her. She would have to find a way to help her friend. Whatever it took, she would do it.

But in the meantime, she had to clear Reacher's name.

She opened the envelope and read about Brad Follett.

When the man on the other end of the bar approached her, she didn't even look up as he arrived.

She simply said, "Go away, please, I'm working."

The man slunk back to his corner of the bar and asked for the check. He was one and done.

Pauling began to read and then her phone rang.

"Hey Tallon," she said, seeing his name on her phone screen.

She listened to him explain about the sniper, ballistics, and finally, Reacher's name.

Pauling never believed in coincidences.

"How soon can you get here?" she asked.

CHAPTER TWENTY-SIX

Rider drove straight to Reese's place, even though he suspected she was dead. From a purely tactical standpoint, however, he believed that she wouldn't have been killed in her home.

He had stopped at a drug store, bought antiseptic and bandages, and stitched up his forearm. The bullet had literally ripped apart his tattoo: a skull breathing fire. It was meant to represent his nickname: the Ghost Rider. He'd gotten it when he was a very young man and always thought about getting it removed.

How appropriate that his enemies had partially taken care of the job for him.

He was fine. He would live and that was all that mattered.

Rider no longer felt any sense of accomplishment or satisfaction. What burned within him now was rage.

As pure and crystalline as the freshly driven snow.

He couldn't stop thinking about the time when he'd been an altar boy in his innocent little hometown and the priest had taken him back into his private quarters after mass. He'd done things to Rider that he simply hadn't understood until much later.

When he had, he'd tracked the priest down and killed him. That had been pretty simple.

Until the shit in Afghanistan had exploded.

And then Reese had saved him.

An angel who'd brought him back to life. More than that, she'd shown him his new mission: to make the men who preyed on the innocent pay.

Rider hung his head.

Now, Reese was dead.

He pulled his rental car up to her apartment building and used a lock pick to get inside. She lived in a modest area of Tribeca. A bit bohemian, perhaps, but full of energy and ideas.

Just like Reese herself.

Once inside, he could see there had been a

struggle. He and Reese had never consummated their relationship, but they'd spent time together. Rider knew the apartment, knew where things belonged.

He thought about Reese and her love of music, food, and life.

But now, there was nothing.

Rider went into her bedroom and looked at her desktop computer. He pulled the keyboard to him, booted it up and saw that it had been wiped clean. The desktop was a blank screen.

He searched 'recent documents' and saw no history. Someone had been very, very thorough.

But Rider knew Reese very well. He found a remote hard drive at the top of her closet. He plugged it into the computer and saw that it contained recordings of the cameras from the apartment.

When the man stepped in, Rider knew him instantly.

Follett.

The sight of the man set his jaw on edge. He ground his teeth and felt blood rage at a level he'd never experienced.

Rider went down to the apartment building's security center and asked to see video of anyone in the parking garage or the street from the last twenty-four hours. Along with the request, he provided a hundred-dollar bill.

Now that he had full cooperation, Rider learned that a street camera guarding the entrance recorded a Range Rover cruising past. Not once. But three times.

There was a visible license plate.

Rider jotted down the plate number and sent a message to a former special ops guy who now worked at the NYPD.

Moments later an address popped up on Rider's phone.

Follett, Rider thought. *Finally*.

Rider got back into his rental car and headed out to Long Island.

CHAPTER TWENTY-SEVEN

The first flight from Las Vegas, the airport nearest Tallon, brought him into New York just before midnight.

He Ubered to Pauling's place and rang the bell.

As he waited for her to buzz him in, a black Cadillac Escalade passed down the street.

Tallon paid it no mind.

Pauling buzzed him in and he took the elevator to her loft.

When she opened the door, he stepped in and kissed her, then licked her lips.

"Mmm," he said. "Have you been drinking gin?"

"Excellent sense of taste," she said. "Yeah, I

had a martini earlier. It's good to see you, by the way."

They bypassed any more discussion and went immediately to the bedroom.

An hour later, they returned to the kitchen and grabbed some leftovers from the fridge, a glass of wine for Pauling, and a beer for Tallon.

"So tell me," Tallon said. "What the hell is going on?"

CHAPTER TWENTY-EIGHT

Jekell parked the Escalade down the street from Pauling's loft.

He checked his pistol – a Glock 10mm and made sure it was loaded. Jekell wasn't an idiot, he knew Pauling's background, as well as Tallon's. He wasn't about to perform a full frontal assault.

That wasn't the point.

In a sense, they were working for him.

Like the very sniper he was pursuing, Jekell just had to be patient. He would let Tallon and Pauling have a short amount of time together, and then they would lead him to the man he pursued.

And then Jekell would kill that man.

If necessary, he would kill Tallon and Pauling too.

Jekell felt no warmth or psychopathic need.

It was just business.

The fact was, the best secrets were buried deep.

And if someone showed up with a shovel, well, they would need to be buried as well.

CHAPTER TWENTY-NINE

Tallon and Pauling pored over the file from Haskins.

"So let me get this straight," Pauling said. "Brad Follett was the CO of a special ops team in Afghanistan. At some point, and there is no official explanation why, the group was disbanded."

Tallon nodded. "Happens all the time," he said. "When there's a problem in a unit, whether it's bad morale, or more often, poor leadership, they basically break the team up and redistribute the individual pieces. If the individuals turn things around, it's usually a sign leadership was bad. Meaning, the issue was systemic and everyone gets a new lease on life, so to speak."

"So it would make sense if Follett fell off the radar after this," Pauling said. It wasn't a statement, more of a question.

"Not really," Tallon said. "The military is usually pretty good at keeping track of people, as long as they're in the service. Once they're out, you can keep tabs on them through their finances – if they're still receiving pay or benefits. If not, only then do they disappear. Off the grid, so to speak – but only if they go all the way."

Pauling studied the thin file.

"Or change their identity."

Tallon nodded. "That, too."

Pauling found nothing in the file. There wasn't much else to go on, other than a single incident report.

"What about this field report about a member of the team who went missing in action? A sniper."

Tallon had noticed that, too.

"It's odd because I was just talking about a sniper in Afghanistan. A legendary guy, really who used a special kind of Russian ammunition called RKN74," Tallon said. "He disappeared. Presumed dead. It wasn't unheard of, at the time."

Pauling studied Tallon's face. "I don't believe

in coincidences." She filled him in on how Haskins had been coerced into getting Pauling involved. "How well do you know your buddy?"

"Brock?" Tallon shrugged. "Pretty well, I guess. When he mentioned Reacher, I thought it was a bit odd."

Tallon picked up the phone and dialed Brock's number. "Hey, how did you come across Reacher's name?" he asked.

Pauling watched as Tallon's eyes narrowed.

"In a text message."

Tallon glanced over at Pauling.

"Okay, roger that."

Tallon hung up.

"Brock says he never sent me a text message about Reacher." Tallon held up his phone. "But it's right here."

Pauling nodded. "Okay, that's some high-tech spook stuff right there. The ability to hijack a phone?"

Tallon nodded. He studied the file.

"Where did this Grim Reaper handle come from?" he asked.

"It was first mentioned in this Army investigation file I got from the Pentagon," Pauling said. "Why?"

"Because the initials G and R make me

curious."

"Tell me more."

"Because the missing sniper? His handle was Ghost Rider."

"That's strange," Pauling said. "What was his real name?"

"Joe. Joe Rider."

Pauling looked back at the file. "It makes sense. He would have been in that unit."

Tallon nodded. "Brad Follett would have been his CO."

"We need to talk to him," Pauling said. "If Follett was the CO, he would have been at the center of the investigation. He would know if Reacher had been involved, if at all. And while we're at it, maybe we can figure out what the hell really happened to Joe Rider."

Tallon wasn't convinced. "I just don't understand if Rider didn't die in Afghanistan, why did he come back and shoot an old guy in Brooklyn?"

Pauling realized she hadn't brought Tallon up to speed on the ballistics. "You heard about the murder of Congressman Ortiz?"

"Yes," Tallon said. "Oh no..."

"Yeah, those ballistics were the same as the old guy in Brooklyn. Same shooter."

"Shit," Tallon said. "We've got to find Follett, and fast."

Pauling held up her phone.

"I'm pulling some strings with my old company. Let's go."

CHAPTER THIRTY

Rider knew he was playing his end game.

When he'd discovered, back in Afghanistan, that Follett was possibly involved in the disappearances of some of the young children, all boys, in the villages they were supposedly protecting, he broke his sniper's silence. There were very few secrets among men fighting side by side in a place like Afghanistan, and word got out quickly.

Rider still wasn't sure how they got to his spotter so quickly and turned him, but they did.

The ambush happened, air support given his coordinates: people died by friendly fire all the time. What was one more dead sniper in the barren mountains of some godforsaken country halfway around the world?

Rider had slowly recovered thanks to Reese and her family, even as Follett's cronies desperately searched for his body. It took him nearly six months to be able to walk again and when he was able to travel, he learned that Follett's unit had been disbanded and his old CO was gone.

Eventually, Rider made it back to the States where he'd gone underground, before rejoining Reese, and creating their new mission.

Together, they'd made the decision to take down Follett's pedophile ring, and hopefully find Follett himself. He'd disappeared since leaving the military, abruptly.

And no one knew where to find him.

Until now.

Rider followed his phone's navigation to a prestigious area of Long Island and pulled around the block from a stunning, contemporary home with an ocean view. He knew Follett loved seaplanes and probably had a hangar somewhere around here.

It was classic Follett, he knew. Showy. Private. But most of all: it was strategic. The home was at the top of a slight rise that sloped down toward the ocean.

Even in hiding, Follett had taken up the position on high ground.

Rider parked his car, double-checked his weapons and circled back to the house.

He weighed his options. Follett would certainly have a top-of-the-line security system, complete with all the bells and whistles like video, motion sensors, maybe even infrared.

At the same time, Follett was no fool. He would know that Rider was on his way, it was why he'd taunted him over the phone. Follett wanted Rider here, to lure him in and kill him once and for all.

Rider was sure Follett intended to finish the job he'd tried to accomplish back in Afghanistan.

The safest play to begin with was the direct approach: Rider went to the front door and found it unlocked.

He smiled.

How nice of Follett to make him feel right at home.

Rider opened the door and stepped inside.

CHAPTER THIRTY-ONE

Detective Claire Brewster had her car's strobe lights flashing as she raced toward Long Island. New Yorkers hated to get out of the way and pretended they had nowhere to go. Claire had no patience with them; she rode their bumpers and jammed herself between vehicles, wishing she could return and ticket all of them for failure to comply.

Things were rocketing ahead faster than Claire had expected: she'd had a warrant assigned to her by a friendly judge, and now she, along with a crash team specifically trained to take down armed fugitives, were headed for the residence of one Brad Follett.

His name had appeared in Victor Panko's

computer files, although it had taken some serious digging by the NYPD's cyber crime division. Not only was Follett's real name eventually discovered, it appeared as if he was the de facto head of the sick little group.

Financial investigators had even tracked down a seaplane in a private hangar that belonged to Follett, who was a licensed pilot. Claire had some theories about why a pedophile and possible psychopath like Follett might want his own plane and the ability to travel incognito, to a certain degree.

If there was one thing in common with sex criminals, they all had a mania for extreme privacy, for obvious reasons.

Claire still wasn't sure who was behind the killing of Panko and Ortiz, but she had a feeling Follett would be at the top of their list and she wanted to get to him before this sniper did.

A bullet to the head, while Follett certainly deserved it, was too easy. Too quick. Claire wanted this Follett guy to be put on trial, to answer to his crimes for all the young lives he'd ruined. He'd taken advantage of wartime orphans, sold them into sex slavery and apparently had a good time doing it.

It had certainly been profitable.

She'd taken a look at the Long Island mansion that matched Follett's address and whistled. It was worth at least a couple million.

Claire wondered if the sniper was already in position.

CHAPTER THIRTY-TWO

Pauling pulled her Mercedes SUV out of the underground parking garage and headed for Long Island. She'd just gotten the address from her old firm's best skip tracer; armed with the new information they'd gotten on Follett, including service record and social security number, linking him to a physical address took her former colleague less than twenty minutes.

As she drove, Pauling didn't notice the black SUV three cars behind her.

"So what do you think happened? Was it another My Lai?" Pauling asked. They still hadn't been able to discover what crime had taken place under Follett's command.

Tallon shook his head. "Not in this day and age," he replied, in response to the idea of a civilian massacre like the one that had happened in Vietnam so many decades ago. Tallon knew My Lai was still used as an educational and training tool – as a perfect example of how failure of leadership can lead to horrific behavior by soldiers.

"Too many cell phones with audio and video," Tallon continued. "I'm not saying it can't happen, but things have changed. So much of warfare now is conducted out in the open, and I'm not talking guns and bombs. I'm talking public relations. Do you remember when that soldier draped an American flag over the fallen statue of Saddam Hussein? All hell broke loose."

"Yeah, the narrative is as important as the war."

They both rode in silence.

"Then what do you think happened?" Pauling asked. "Afghanistan is full of heroin – maybe they were involved in drug dealing. Shipping stuff back home. Or maybe murder on a smaller level. What if this Joe Rider went crazy and shot a bunch of people?"

"It's certainly possible," Tallon said. "But it doesn't fit for me. From what I'd heard Rider was a true sniper: dedicated. A ghost. Serious about his profession. Guys like that usually don't go off the deep end."

"No? What about the old man in Brooklyn and Congressman Ortiz?"

Tallon looked out the windows as they left the city. "I don't have an answer for that. All I can tell you is the guys who usually go off the deep end are the undisciplined ones who get sloppy and careless and have serious, underlying issues," he said. "If anything, a guy like Rider might have witnessed something he shouldn't have, and someone disappeared him."

"Now that makes way more sense."

"But if it was Rider who's been shooting civilians back here…"

The unspoken thought hung in the air.

"Maybe Follett can shed some light on all of this," Pauling said.

"Maybe," Tallon said. He was looking at his side view mirror. There had been a black SUV behind them, but now, it was gone.

"Here we are," Pauling said as she pulled up to the house. There were no cars in the driveway and no obvious signs someone was home.

There were sirens in the distance.

"Locked and loaded?" Tallon asked her.

"Let's go," she said and headed for the front door.

CHAPTER THIRTY-THREE

During his time in active service, Follett wasn't a sniper. He was a crack shot with both a rifle and a pistol, but the long gun hadn't been his primary weapon.

As a CO, snipers had been under his command and he had worked closely with many of them in the field, including Joe Rider.

Rider was the best he'd ever seen.

A ghost.

The problem was, Rider was also one of those holier-than-thou kind of guys. Always pretending to think of others, there to save the world.

It was all bullshit, Follett thought. The only thing that mattered in this life was getting yours before you died. It didn't matter what you wanted, but what was the point of helping others?

When you died, no one would remember the good things you'd done.

Follett had spent his life acquiring things he desired, be it young boys, fancy toys or ocean-front property. That guiding desire had never done him wrong.

And right now, all he wanted was to put a bullet through Joe Rider's head. Follett had suspected back in Afghanistan that the ambush hadn't been successful. But the Ghost had slipped away.

Well, he wouldn't make the same mistake twice.

Snipers were all about precision, patience and camouflage. Follett also had the advantage of firsthand knowledge of the battlefield; it was his home after all. When he had taunted Rider after killing the Afghani girl, Follett knew the sniper would track him down and try to kill him.

Follett utilized his familiarity with the house and it's L-shape, designed to maximize ocean views from every room. His master bedroom included a balcony at one end of the L that provided an overhang with a full view of the great room.

Follett had chosen his own rifle, chambered with Rider's favorite RKN74 ammo as a bit of poetic justice. Nothing in his life was ever done without first thinking how to maximize pleasure from the action.

He'd already seen a shadow in the great room and knew it was Rider. This was because his home alarm system included a video feed linked directly to his phone. So he'd been able to see Rider enter the house.

Now, Follett was tempted to check his phone but he didn't want to miss his shot, either.

The key was the kitchen. It sported a huge breakfast bar and anyone entering the home looking to kill its owner would certainly approach the marble-topped partition and look behind it. When Rider did that, Follett would blow his head off.

He just had to be patient.

CHAPTER THIRTY-FOUR

High ground.

Rider weighed what he knew of Follett and the layout of the house. He also knew that Follett's ego was about the same size as this Long Island mansion, maybe even a little larger.

He would want to beat Rider at his own game.

Which meant most likely that Follett had taken the high ground. When he'd driven past, Rider had noted the angles of the house, the overall L-shape designed to give views from every window, along with various porches and balconies, particularly the one on the south end of the house.

The security cameras were visible, too. So when he entered, Rider had gone straight away from the kitchen to a mud room. It consisted of a short hallway with rows of cubbies on the left, and hooks for coats on the right. The hooks were empty, as were the shelves.

It didn't look like Follett spent a lot of time at the house.

Rider stopped short of actually entering the space, though, because there was a camera trained at the back door. It was positioned in the corner of the hall's doorway, which meant its blind spot ended a few feet into the room.

It was why Rider had stopped as he was now just behind the camera. He simply pulled out his short folding knife, reached up and neatly sliced the cable at the rear of the camera.

And then he walked out the back door.

He quickly circled around the house until he reached the corner of the southern end of the L.

Rider dropped to the ground with his rifle in hand. He slowly pulled himself along the wet grass until he could just see the edge of the balcony.

What he saw was a gift: Follett was prone on the deck of the balcony, looking down into the great room.

Rider brought his rifle to his shoulder.

The balcony was made of plank decking, with

a modern railing. A patch of Follett's head was just visible through two rows of the railing's cables.

Rider heard sirens and could see through the great room window that someone else was coming through the front door.

He had to take the shot, and take it now.

Rider's finger tightened on the trigger.

He put the crosshairs on the back of Follett's head.

He let out an easy breath, slowly squeezed the trigger and then everything went black.

CHAPTER THIRTY-FIVE

Pauling heard the sound of two gunshots coming from behind the house. She was already inside, heading for the kitchen, but Tallon had circled to the back.

She turned to run and provide cover for Tallon, but saw through the window as a stream of police cars roared into the driveway.

A woman emerged from the first car – an unmarked with lights flashing from the car's grill. A detective, no doubt.

From behind her, a group of cops fanned out, all wearing blue jackets and bulletproof vests.

They would get to Tallon before she could.

Pauling put her pistol on the kitchen counter and stepped outside with her hands in the air.

A third gunshot sounded.

Tallon, she thought.

CHAPTER THIRTY-SIX

For a big man, Jekell moved with the kind of physical grace that had served him well over the years. People never expected a man of his size could be so light on his feet.

He'd parked the black Escalade on the other side of the Long Island mansion, after seeing Pauling and Tallon park to the west. Then, he'd been able to slip into the backyard just as he saw Rider come through the house's back door.

Jekell hadn't moved a muscle, not even a twitch.

He knew all too well what Rider was capable of.

It had been Jekell's job to make Rider disappear back in Afghanistan, and he'd failed. As a private contractor frequently employed by the CIA, it was the only blemish on his resumé.

Jekell had never lost to anyone in the field, and he'd made it his mission to track down Rider. He had no idea why anyone had wanted the man killed in the first place, but as long as the sniper was still loose, Jekell's credibility to clients was shattered.

It was why he'd put together a plan: find the original investigator who'd worked the case. The name Jack Reacher had come up, but no one could find him. However, a former FBI agent turned private investigator had ties to Reacher. And, she worked frequently with a former special ops soldier named Michael Tallon.

They'd been the perfect team for Jekell to exploit.

And now, finally, he had Rider in his crosshairs, not the other way around.

Jekell watched the sniper go to the ground and slowly bring his rifle to bear.

At last, Jekell moved and walked slowly toward Rider, his Glock aimed at the man's head. He could tell Rider was about to fire.

Jekell's finger tightened on the trigger and just as he fired, Rider fired, too.

CHAPTER THIRTY-SEVEN

Tallon's years in combat provided him the ability to take in information rapidly and process it with reflex-like speed.

He'd come around the corner of the house after exiting the back door and saw two things simultaneously: the black Cadillac Escalade he'd seen behind them on the highway, and now, a man dressed in black with a pistol in his hand.

Tallon noted the Glock, the tension in the man's body and knew he was about to fire. The target wasn't visible, as the man was aiming at something around the corner of the house.

The man fired.

Tallon saw the big man's wrists flex with the

recoil and then with shocking quickness and in a fluid motion, he wheeled on Tallon.

"No," Tallon said. His own gun was in his hand as the man's gun came in line.

Everything slowed down for Tallon. The man had followed them. He'd been after the same quarry, which meant the shooter now facing him had planned to deal with he and Pauling.

It all raced through Tallon's mind with breathtaking clarity. They'd been used to flush out the game.

And now, the man was going to retire them, too.

The big man's gun didn't waver and a small smile tugged at the corner of his mouth.

"Put it down," Tallon said.

But the man's finger tightened on the trigger, so Tallon fired three times fast, all center mass.

The big man got off one shot that crashed into a window somewhere behind Tallon's head.

It seemed to happen in slow motion: the big man took a slight step forward, the gun fell from his hands and then he slowly fell forward, crashing face first into the ground.

Tallon knew he was dead before he hit the ground.

Suddenly, there were a half-dozen cops in

matching blue windbreakers fanning out around Tallon.

"Put it down," they said.

Unlike the dead man on the ground, Tallon followed orders.

CHAPTER THIRTY-EIGHT

Detective Claire Brewster stood next to Pauling and Tallon. They were both in handcuffs although Claire had verified they were, in fact, who they said they were. She didn't care much for private investigators and right now, they were the least of her concerns.

They stood over the big, dead man dressed all in black. The home's owner, Brad Follett, also deceased, had already been identified.

"Who is he?" Tallon asked, lifting his chin toward the dead man.

Brewster looked back at him. "How the hell should I know? You're the one who killed him."

Tallon had to admit, she had a point.

Together, they walked to the edge of the

house and Tallon saw a pool of blood on the grass. A rifle lay next to the blood.

But there was no body.

Tallon glanced at Pauling who nodded back at him.

Rider.

The Ghost.

He'd done it again.

CHAPTER THIRTY-NINE

They spent nearly a full day in an interrogation room in the bowels of the NYPD before Pauling's attorney finally sprung them both.

There were no pending charges against Tallon, as the shooting was clearly in self-defense. Follett's security system also had a camera covering the rear of the property and they'd all been able to see the man now identified as Steven Jekell refuse to comply.

The detective, Brewster, had finally told them off the record, of course, that Jekell had been an ex-CIA operative with a fairly long rap sheet. In fact, there was more than one current investigation into his team for their work overseas.

However, those probes hadn't resulted in any

kind of restrictions on his access to the DOD's technology. Once his identity had been verified, Brewster's team had gone to an office in Virginia where they'd arrested a colleague of Jekell's named Foley, and confiscated all of their computers, weapons and equipment. It had clearly been a black-ops unit, with ties to multiple international incidents.

"He was no doubt involved in the ambush that tried to kill Rider in the first place," Pauling said.

"Guys like him would consider it a stain on his record," Tallon pointed out. "Unfinished business that probably gnawed at him and maybe even cost him contracts. Money and pride to a guy like Jekell are everything."

Claire sipped from a Styrofoam cup of coffee. "He's small potatoes. Follett is the real deal. I wish this Rider guy hadn't blown his head off, because it would have been good to interrogate him. But we're getting loads of evidence, mostly from his plane."

"His plane?" Pauling asked.

"Yeah," Claire replied. "Follett liked to do most of his dirty work in a seaplane. Flying around anonymously, parking in the middle of the ocean somewhere in order to do his dirty work in private."

"Great place to dispose of bodies, too," Tallon said.

"We've got video," Claire said. "Makes you sick to see."

Pauling's attorney waved them toward the door.

"I wonder where Rider is now," Pauling said, ignoring the gesture. She kind of liked this Claire Brewster. The woman seemed like a straight shooter.

Tallon shrugged his shoulders.

"We have no idea, at the moment," Claire said. "I still have no idea how the hell he slipped through our fingers. There was maybe a ten-second window…"

"That's all a guy like Rider needs," Tallon said.

Steam from Claire's coffee rose into the air and disappeared.

CHAPTER FORTY

Rider looked at himself in the mirror.

It wasn't a pretty sight.

The bullet from Jekell's pistol had plowed its way across his forehead before careening off his skull. Now, there was a three-inch gash in his forehead and a chunk of flesh missing. The area around it was swollen and bruised.

It was ugly.

But at least he was still alive.

Rider knew he had his rifle to thank for that. Once again, it had saved his life.

The RKN74 round was a powerful bullet. Even with his custom-fitted rifle the recoil was impressive. When he fired the shot that blew apart Follett's head, the kick from his rifle jolted his head and shoulder back an inch or two.

The beauty of it all was that he, Rider, must have fired a hare's breath before Jekell pulled the trigger.

While Rider's shot found its intended target with deadly accuracy, Jekell's was off by a matter of inches because Rider's head jerked backward.

If Jekell had fired a moment earlier, the bullet probably would have hit him square in the side of the head and it would have been the end of him.

Death by head shot.

Instead, the bullet had slammed along the top of his forehead, peeling off a chunk of flesh and momentarily knocking him unconscious.

When he'd come to an instant later, he'd done what always came naturally: he simply disappeared into the trees separating Follett's house from his neighbors. From there, he'd worked backward, using his sniper's gift of camouflage to eventually leave Long Island.

Now, in the cheap hotel room he studied the gash on his forehead. He thought of Reese and how happy she would be that he'd been able to fulfill their mission. The man who'd been responsible for tearing the life and soul out of her village was finally dead.

Justice, delivered RKN74 style.

Rider winced as he doused his wound with antiseptic. There would be a scar for certain and it wouldn't be pretty.

That was okay, he reasoned.

To most people, he was practically invisible.

BUY THE NEXT BOOK IN THE SERIES

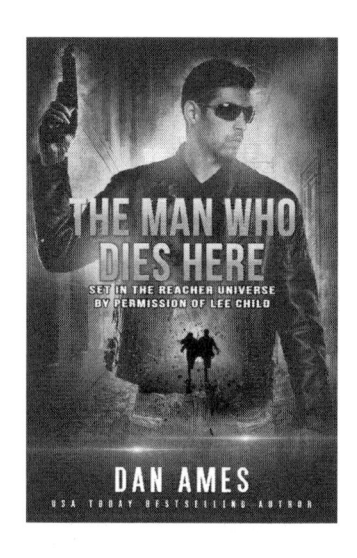

Book #16 in The JACK REACHER Cases

A FAST-PACED ACTION-PACKED THRILLER SERIES

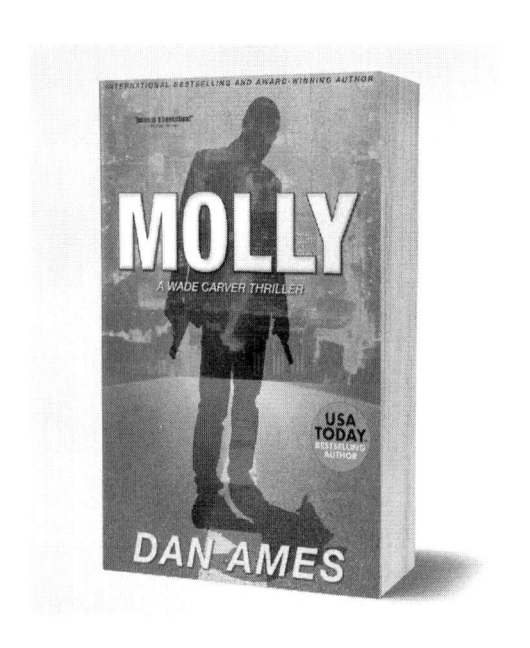

AN AWARD-WINNING BESTSELLING MYSTERY SERIES

Buy DEAD WOOD, the first John Rockne Mystery.

"Fast-paced, engaging, original."
-*NYTimes bestselling author Thomas Perry*

ABOUT THE AUTHOR

Dan Ames is a USA TODAY Bestselling Author, Amazon Kindle #1 bestseller, GoodReads Readers Choice finalist and winner of the Independent Book Award for Crime Fiction.

www.authordanames.com
dan@authordanames.com

ALSO BY DAN AMES

THE JACK REACHER CASES

The JACK REACHER Cases #1 (A Hard Man To Forget)

The JACK REACHER Cases #2 (The Right Man For Revenge)

The JACK REACHER Cases #3 (A Man Made For Killing)

The JACK REACHER Cases #4 (The Last Man To Murder)

The JACK REACHER Cases #5 (The Man With No Mercy)

The JACK REACHER Cases #6 (A Man Out For Blood)

The JACK REACHER Cases #7 (A Man Beyond The Law)

The JACK REACHER Cases #8 (The Man Who Walks Away)

The JACK REACHER Cases (The Man Who Strikes Fear)

The JACK REACHER Cases (The Man Who Stands Tall)

The JACK REACHER Cases (The Man Who Works Alone)

The Jack Reacher Cases (A Man Built For Justice)

The JACK REACHER Cases #13 (A Man Born for Battle)

The JACK REACHER Cases #14 (The Perfect Man for Payback)

The JACK REACHER Cases #15 (The Man Whose Aim Is True)

The JACK REACHER Cases #16 (The Man Who Dies Here)

The JACK REACHER Cases #17 (The Man With Nothing To Lose)

The JACK REACHER Cases #18 (The Man Who Never Goes Back)

The JACK REACHER Cases #19 (The Man From The Shadows)

The JACK REACHER CASES #20 (The Man Behind The Gun)

JACK REACHER'S SPECIAL INVESTIGATORS

BOOK ONE: DEAD MEN WALKING

BOOK TWO: GAME OVER

BOOK THREE: LIGHTS OUT

BOOK FOUR: NEVER FORGIVE, NEVER FORGET

BOOK FIVE: HIT THEM FAST, HIT THEM HARD

BOOK SIX: FINISH THE FIGHT

THE JOHN ROCKNE MYSTERIES

DEAD WOOD (John Rockne Mystery #1)
HARD ROCK (John Rockne Mystery #2)
COLD JADE (John Rockne Mystery #3)
LONG SHOT (John Rockne Mystery #4)
EASY PREY (John Rockne Mystery #5)
BODY BLOW (John Rockne Mystery #6)

THE WADE CARVER THRILLERS

MOLLY (Wade Carver Thriller #1)
SUGAR (Wade Carver Thriller #2)
ANGEL (Wade Carver Thriller #3)

THE WALLACE MACK THRILLERS

THE KILLING LEAGUE (Wallace Mack Thriller #1)

THE MURDER STORE (Wallace Mack Thriller #2)

FINDERS KILLERS (Wallace Mack Thriller #3)

THE MARY COOPER MYSTERIES

DEATH BY SARCASM (Mary Cooper Mystery #1)

MURDER WITH SARCASTIC INTENT (Mary Cooper Mystery #2)

GROSS SARCASTIC HOMICIDE (Mary Cooper Mystery #3)

THE CIRCUIT RIDER (WESTERNS)

THE CIRCUIT RIDER (Circuit Rider #1)
KILLER'S DRAW (Circuit Rider #2)

THE RAY MITCHELL THRILLERS

THE RECRUITER

KILLING THE RAT

HEAD SHOT

STANDALONE THRILLERS:

KILLER GROOVE (Rockne & Cooper Mystery #1)

BEER MONEY (Burr Ashland Mystery #1)

TO FIND A MOUNTAIN (A WWII Thriller)

BOX SETS:

AMES TO KILL

GROSSE POINTE PULP

GROSSE POINTE PULP 2

TOTAL SARCASM

WALLACE MACK THRILLER COLLECTION

SHORT STORIES:

THE GARBAGE COLLECTOR

BULLET RIVER

SCHOOL GIRL

HANGING CURVE

SCALE OF JUSTICE

FREE BOOKS AND MORE

Would you like a FREE copy of my story BULLET RIVER and the chance to win a free Kindle?

Then sign up for the DAN AMES BOOK CLUB:

AUTHORDANAMES.COM

Printed in Great Britain
by Amazon